ALETÍN AND THE FALLING SKY

Mizca ayím acalologaec, ajím conogdac, ajím conogdac.
I am not timid, I am brave, I am brave.

Mocoví chant

Aletín and the Falling Sky is based on an unnamed myth included in *Historia de la Conquista del Paraguay,* by Jose Guevara. Buenos Aires: 1882.

This story is from the Mocoví of Argentina.

Library of Congress Cataloging-in-Publication Data

Lilly, Melinda.
    Aletín and the falling sky / retold by Melinda Lilly;   illustrated by Charles Reasoner.
        p. cm.—(Latin American tales and myths)
    Summary: When the falling Sky causes the Sun to crash to the Earth, Aletín saves the situation and finds that his people and their world have been changed forever.
    ISBN 1-57103-262-2
    1. Mocobí Indians—Folklore. 2.Tales—Argentina. [1. Mocobí Indians—Folklore. 2. Indians of South Africa—Argentina—Folklore. 3. Folklore—Argentina.]
I. Reasoner, Charles, ill. II. Title III.Series: Lilly, Melinda. Latin American tales and myths.
F2823.M6L55 1999
398.2'089'98082—dc21

99-12100
CIP
AC

Printed in the USA

Latin American Tales and Myths

ALETÍN
AND THE FALLING SKY

A Mocoví Myth

Retold by
Melinda Lilly

Illustrated by
Charles Reasoner

The Rourke Press, Inc.
Vero Beach, Florida 32964

Aletín peeked open one eye and looked over the condition of the world. Sun was still hanging in the sky baking the thirsty grasslands. The palm trees that supported Aletín's hammock continued to stand tall. A slow breeze was tickling the treetops. The river in the distance followed the same course; it hadn't stopped flowing or changed direction while Aletín had slept. Everything was the same as before his short nap. He breathed a sigh of relief. "Perhaps this will be a good day," he hoped. "A day without troubles, a day when nothing happens."

4

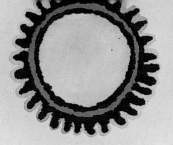

In Aletín's time, when Earth was fresh and new, it was an unfinished, unruly, and unpredictable place. In those early days, the world was populated by plants and a few villagers, nothing else. Animals lived only in people's imaginations and a steady, reliable world seemed an impossible dream.

But not to Aletín. He believed that if he kept fixing the world, someday it would come right and days would calmly follow nights, one after the other. Then maybe he could get some rest. Although all the villagers tidied up Earth, Aletín worked most faithfully to help it overcome its growing pains. He trained the trees to grow up instead of down, coaxed the rivers back within their banks, and convinced the clouds to drop rain instead of keeping it all for themselves.

After looking over the skyline one more time, Aletín hopped out of his hammock. Something wasn't right. He looked up at Sun hanging motionless in the heavens. "Dazoá Sun, have you forgotten where to go to rest?" he asked patiently. "We've had sunlight for day, after day, after day. It's long past time for sunset. The plants are wilting and my villagers and I want to sleep in the darkness." Sun seemed lost, not able to tell down from up or sunrise from sunset.

"I will help you find your hammock below Earth," said Aletín. "You probably need rest too, Sun, my friend." He picked up his throwing stick and balanced it in his hand, thinking of a plan to bring on the night. "Follow my stick," he told Sun. "It will show you where you need to go." He aimed for the western horizon, twirling his stick overhead. He ran through the tall grass and then hurled his stick as hard as he could.

Holding his breath with hopeful anticipation, he watched as it skimmed over thorn bushes and past tall palm trees that scratched the hot bleached sky. It bounced at the edge of the flat South American grasslands and pierced the smooth seam that divided the land from the air. His throwing stick had stuck in the horizon!

"Dazoá Sun, slide down past my stick and bring on the
sunset," ordered Aletín. Relieved to finally know where to go,
Sun slid out of the western sky as impatient Cidaigo Moon
popped upward.

Aletín retrieved his stick from the seam of the horizon and headed back home, happy at his success. He dashed around palm trees, his black hair flying behind him. "Cidaigo Moon! Naadic Milky Way! I travel in the sky with you!" he sang. Moon glowed brightly and Milky Way sparkled.

He raced once around the palm trees that held his hammock and then dove into it, swinging. All was right with the world again, what a relief! As the swinging hammock slowed to stillness, he curled up, ready to sleep through the night for the first time in many days.

KRIIIIP! The deafening sound of something ripping shook the forest. Aletín opened his eyes and warily glanced around. A high, toneless whistle caused him to look up. "Oh no," he muttered, slowly shaking his head. There, dangling above him, was a small pale star studded with shining points. It whistled forlornly, flashing and sputtering with light as it swung back and forth on a dark piece of torn sky.

"Stay up there!" Aletín commanded, pushing himself out of his hammock. His voice softened as he asked, "Little Amanic Star, can't you swing over and poke yourself back into the evening sky?" The star made no response. It simply sagged at the end of a jagged hole that reached midway down the trunks of the palm trees.

With a squeak, Star fell onto the hammock and gently glowed. Aletín took a vine and formed it into a sling. Then he picked two palm fronds off of the ground. Using them as giant hands, he carefully lifted jagged Amanic Star out of the hammock and into the vine sling. He draped it over his shoulder and looked for footholds on the palm tree.

Star bounced against Aletín's back as he shimmied up the tree's slender trunk and onto the crown of palm leaves. Standing on tiptoe, he ran his fingers along the tear in the night. As soft as a moth's wing, it fluttered when he jabbed it twice with the point of his stick. He threaded the rope sling through the small holes and stitched the star back to the sky.

Amanic Star cast a shimmering glow of gratitude on Aletín as he slipped down into his hammock, stretched, and yawned. "What a day and day and day and evening this has been," he mused. "Tonight I will dream of a peaceful, boring world," he promised himself and closed his eyes.

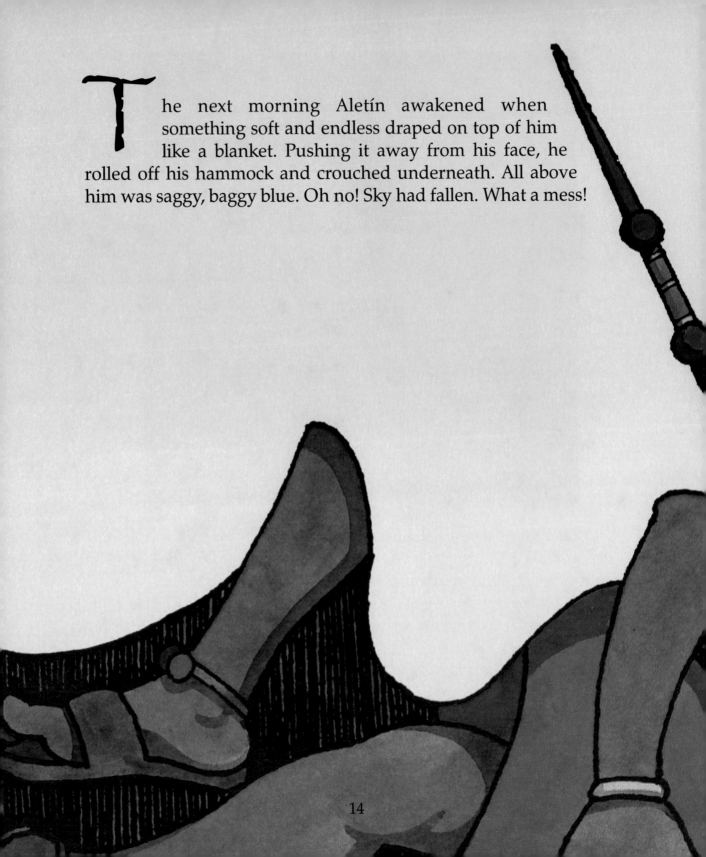

The next morning Aletín awakened when something soft and endless draped on top of him like a blanket. Pushing it away from his face, he rolled off his hammock and crouched underneath. All above him was saggy, baggy blue. Oh no! Sky had fallen. What a mess!

Aletín slowly shook his head, then leaned out from under the hammock and gently poked the sky. "Don't be a lazy layabout, Ypequim Sky!" he scolded. "Rise up! Go back where you belong! Up! Up!" Sky just sagged.

Aletín crawled out from under the hammock and listened for the sounds of his neighbors. Hearing muffled cries, he headed toward them, pushing aside Sky as though swimming. One by one he found and helped untangle his villagers. Making a chain of people, they pushed their way beneath a cluster of tall palm trees and sat in the small open area.

"There's no place for us anymore," cried a thin woman, covering her eyes with her painted hands. "Sky leaves us no room to even move!"

"This is the end of the world!" wailed a tall, tattooed man, pulling a soggy cloud from his hair.

"This isn't the end. Maybe it's a new beginning," said Aletín in a quiet, reassuring voice. He looked into his people's eyes, trying to share his feelings of hope. "We can bunch Sky on top of our huts, pile it on our hammocks, throw it in the river. Come! We must try."

Aletín's words fell on their ears like a fresh rain. They lifted their heads, wiped away their doubts, and began to work together. The tall, tattooed man held the heavens in his outstretched hands.

The strongest people propped it up by raising long tree branches. The children blew away the clouds. Despite all these efforts, there was still too much Sky drooping everywhere.

Not only that, the villagers grew tired under its weight. The tall and the strong began to stoop. The children ran out of breath. Squinting and shading his eyes, Aletín wearily eyed Sun. Although it looked squished, it was the only thing big enough to hold up the rest of the sagging Sky. "We've got to throw Sky on top of Dazoá Sun!" Aletín urged.

Flexing their sore muscles once again, the villagers tossed Sky into the air. "Ooof!" Breathing hard, they hopped, bouncing it off their fingertips. It rose up and up. With the last of their strength, the people leaped as high as they could, pushing it up and over toward Sun. With a loud *WHUMP!* it landed right on top of Dazoá Sun.

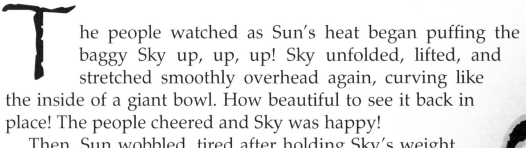

The people watched as Sun's heat began puffing the baggy Sky up, up, up! Sky unfolded, lifted, and stretched smoothly overhead again, curving like the inside of a giant bowl. How beautiful to see it back in place! The people cheered and Sky was happy!

Then, Sun wobbled, tired after holding Sky's weight. With a fiery flash, Sun slipped down out of the heavens with a thud!

"Now what?" thought Aletín.

Sun skidded on the seam of the horizon and rolled onto Earth! The grasslands exploded with flames as Sun rolled and rolled!

The people ran. Sun rolled downhill,
coming closer, coming faster. Some
people raced toward the wide river, their
feet flying over the burning ground. They leaped into
the water. Sun licked the river's edge, making the water
spit, bubble, and boil. Shapes emerged from the steam—the
people turned into amazing creatures never seen before.
They became fish with flashing scales, alligators with skin
toughened by fire, water bugs colored by smoke, and
ducks with dark feathers.

Dazoá Sun continued rolling downhill through the forest, lighting palm trees like torches. In the veil of smoke people ran and climbed, turning into jaguars with spots of ash on their coats and monkeys swinging through the tall trees. A few burrowed in the dirt and became toads, armadillos, or anteaters as rolling Sun passed over them.

Aletín did not want to swim, run, climb, or hide. He was not afraid. He knew what he had to do. When Sun came to him, he threw his stick into the air and didn't let go. The stick pulled him up and they flew as one, transforming into a toucan with long, sunlit wings.

Aletín Toucan looked down, seeing people running to their huts. Rolling Sun chased them, trapping them in their houses. Aletín had to stop Sun before it hurt his people! He dove, drew back his head, and stabbed burning Sun with his great beak. Fire! Fire! It was so hot! Frantically flapping his powerful wings, he lifted Sun off the ground. He flew straight up to the outstretched Sky and poked Dazoá Sun back into the heavens.

The people came out of their huts cheering, "Aletín Cotaá! Aletín Toucan!" He circled above them waving his beak, now brightly colored from Sun's fire.

"You too have been changed by Sun," he cried. "Now you are the mighty Mocoví people!"

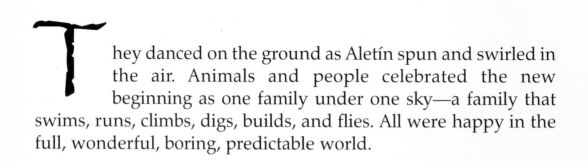

They danced on the ground as Aletín spun and swirled in the air. Animals and people celebrated the new beginning as one family under one sky—a family that swims, runs, climbs, digs, builds, and flies. All were happy in the full, wonderful, boring, predictable world.

PRONUNCIATION AND DEFINITION GUIDE

Aletín (ah lay TEEN) — the name of a Mocoví young man

amanic (ah MAH neek) — Mocoví for the Southern Cross constellation or a star from that constellation; also, Mocoví for rhea, a large, flightless South American bird

cidaigo (see DIE goh) — Mocoví for moon

cotaá (koh tah AH) — Mocoví for toucan

dazoá (dah soh AH) — Mocoví for sun

Gran Chaco (gran CHAW coh) — The great grassland plain of central South America, the Gran Chaco is prone to long droughts broken by seasonal floods.

hammock (HAM uk) — a hanging bed made of netting

Mocoví (moh koh VEE) — a culture and people of the plains of the Argentinian Gran Chaco and their language; after the introduction of horses, the Mocoví became known for their skill as riders.

naadic (NAH deek) — Mocoví for Milky Way

ypequim (yip ae GEEM) — Mocoví for sky